This book belongs to

· · · · · · · · · · · · · · · · · · · ·

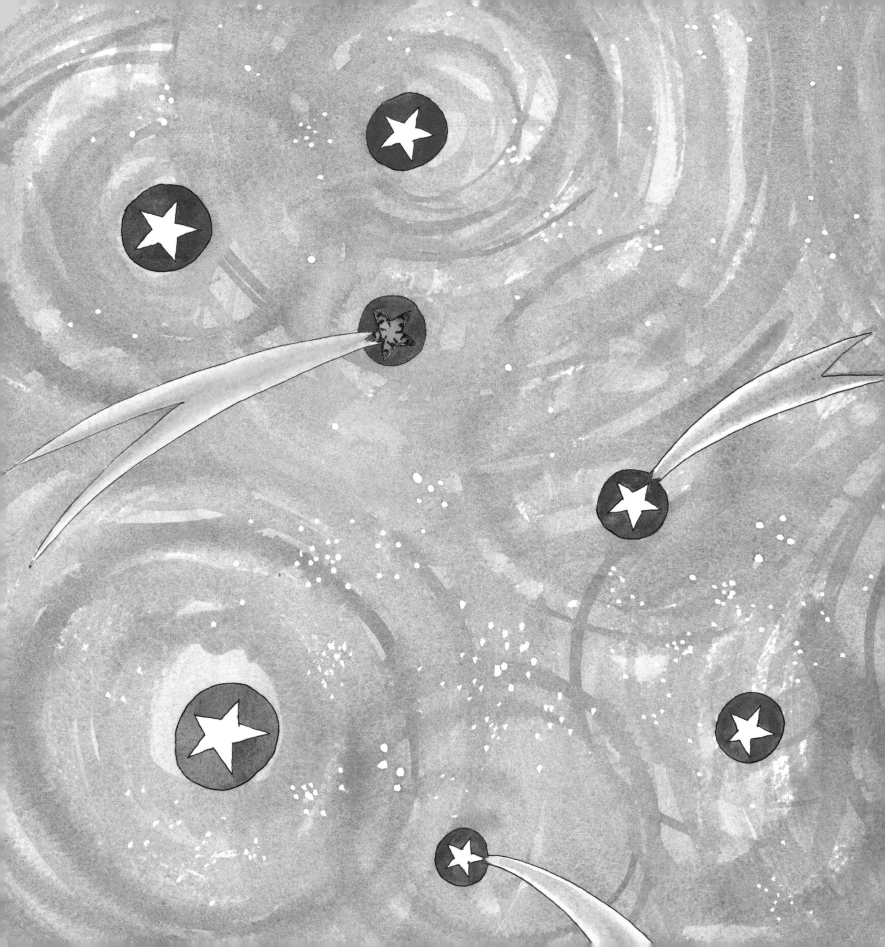

where did that

for all the Earth babies –
every one a star
D.G.

WHERE DID THAT BABY COME FROM?
A PICTURE CORGI BOOK 0 552 55035 3

First published in Great Britain by Doubleday,
an imprint of Random House Children's Books

Doubleday edition published 2004
Picture Corgi edition published 2005

1 3 5 7 9 10 8 6 4 2

Copyright © Debi Gliori, 2004
Designed by Ian Butterworth

Picture Corgi Books are published by Random House Children's Books,
61–63 Uxbridge Road, London W5 5SA,
a division of The Random House Group Ltd,
in Australia by Random House Australia (Pty) Ltd,
20 Alfred Street, Milsons Point, Sydney, NSW 2061, Australia,
in New Zealand by Random House New Zealand Ltd,
18 Poland Road, Glenfield, Auckland 10, New Zealand,
and in South Africa by Random House (Pty) Ltd,
Endulini, 5A Jubilee Road, Parktown 2193, South Africa

THE RANDOM HOUSE GROUP Limited Reg. No. 954009
www.**kids**at**randomhouse**.co.uk

A CIP catalogue record for this book is available from the British Library.

Printed in Singapore

baby come from ?

Debi Gliori

PICTURE CORGI

Where did that baby come from,
and can we take it back?
It wails and squeaks, its nappy leaks —
it's an insomniac.

W here did that baby come from,

did it float down from the sky?

It's got no wings or feathered things —

I don't think it can fly.

Where did that baby come from,
did it grow out of a seed?
Will roses grow between its toes
or is it just a weed?

Where did that baby come from,
did you buy it in a store?
Amongst the lots of bargain tots —
please don't buy any more.

SPECI
OFFER
free ~ range
babies

Where did that baby come from,
did you find it at the zoo?
You didn't heed the 'Please don't feed'
but brought it home with you.

Where did that baby come from,
did you build it from a kit?
All it can do is pee and poo —
Does it have a missing bit?

Where did that baby come from,
did you bake it like a bun?
Yeuchh - take a look - it's not quite cooked —
don't make another one.

Where did that baby come from,
did you fish it out the sea?
It doesn't swim, it has no fins —
come on, let's set it free.

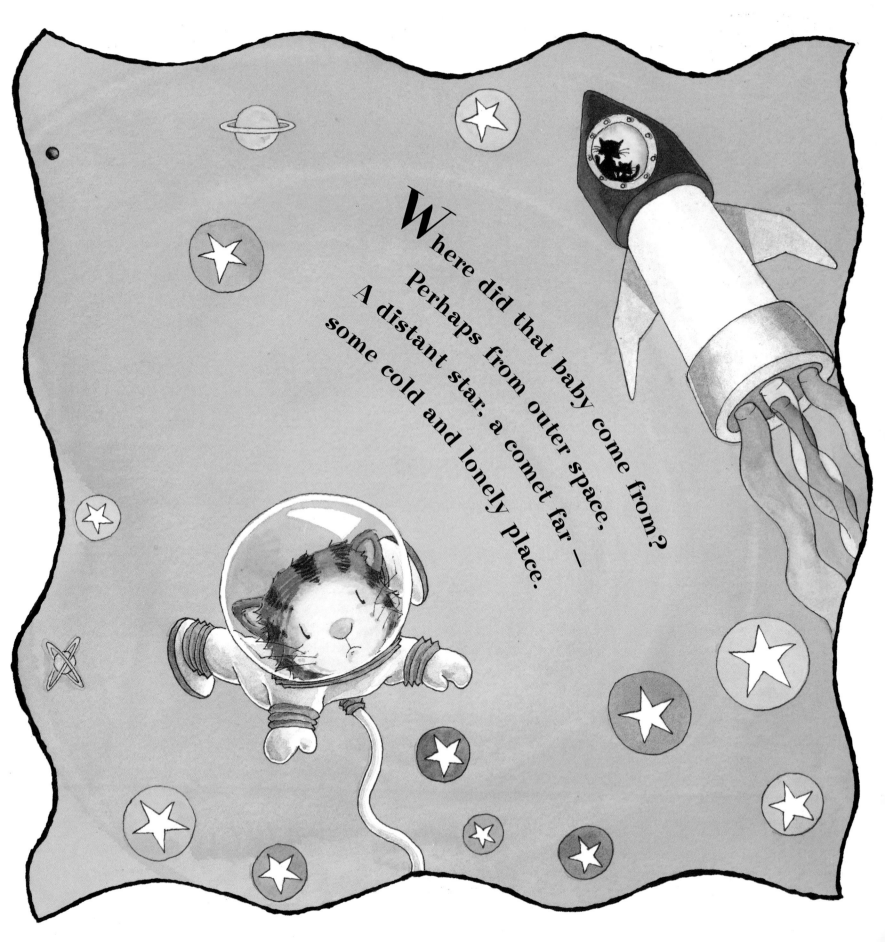

Where did that baby come from?
Perhaps from outer space,
A distant star, a comet far —
some cold and lonely place.

Why is that baby crying?
Oh, baby, why d'you weep?
I'll keep you warm and safe from harm
and help you fall asleep.

Baby, why are you laughing?
Was it something that I said?
A peek-a-boo, or I-love-you,
a kiss dropped on your head?

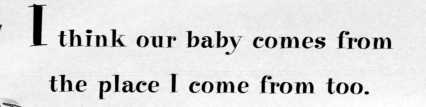

I think our baby comes from
the place I come from too.

Our place of birth was planet Earth,

this baby, me ... and you.

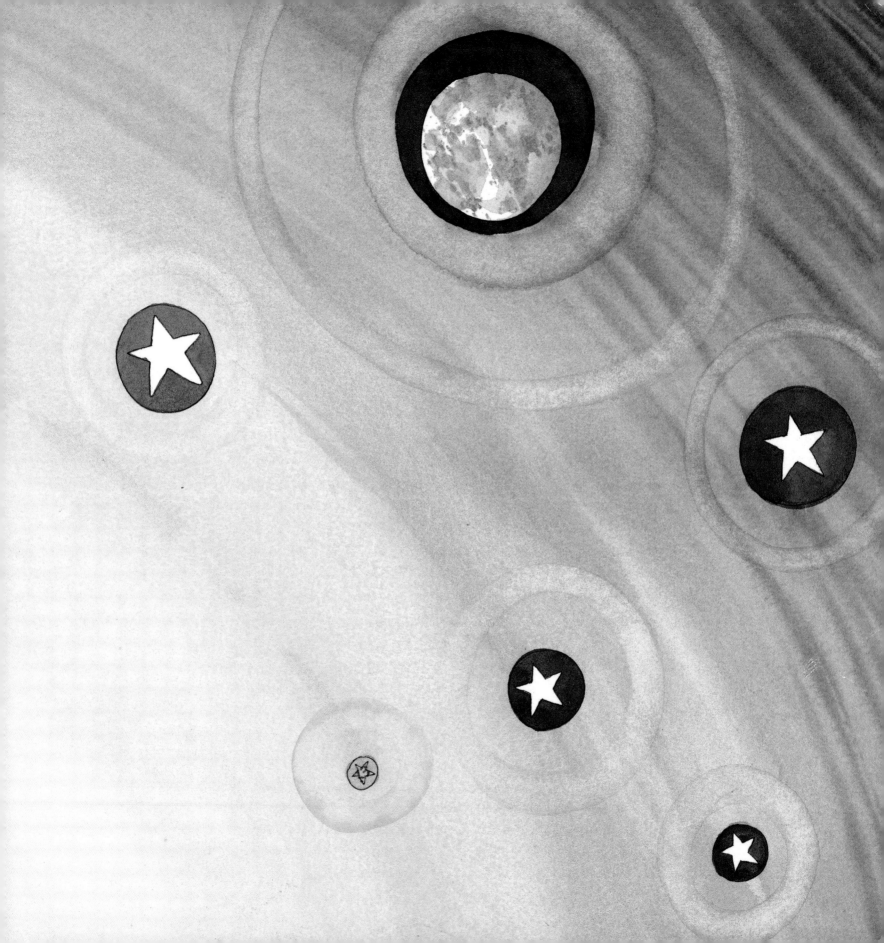

Also by Debi Gliori:

Penguin Post

★

Always and Forever
written by Alan Durant

★

Tell Me Something Happy Before I Go To Sleep
written by Joyce Dunbar

★

Tell Me What It's Like To Be Big
written by Joyce Dunbar

★

The Very Small
written by Joyce Dunbar